Geo Oliver

Plain Facts on Vaccination

Anatiposi

Geo Oliver

Plain Facts on Vaccination

Reprint of the original.

1st Edition 2023 | ISBN: 978-3-38210-212-8

Anatiposi Verlag is an imprint of Outlook Verlagsgesellschaft mbH.

Verlag (Publisher): Outlook Verlag GmbH, Zeilweg 44, 60439 Frankfurt, Deutschland
Vertretungsberechtigt (Authorized to represent): E. Roepke, Zeilweg 44, 60439 Frankfurt, Deutschland
Druck (Print): Books on Demand GmbH, In de Tarpen 42, 22848 Norderstedt, Deutschland

PLAIN FACTS

ON

VACCINATION:

BY

GEO. OLIVER, M.B. (IN HONOURS) LOND: &c.

⁕⁕⁕

LONDON:
SIMPKIN, MARSHALL, AND CO.

DARLINGTON: REDCAR:
W. DRESSER.   G. F. BATES.

—

1871.

"The keenest of all arguments for or against the practice of Vaccination will be *those which are engraven with the point of the lancet.*"

JENNER.

The Author proposes to issue shortly a brief summary (suitable for general distribution,) of the principal facts contained in this publication, in the hope it may be useful to Public Vaccinators and others desirous of removing fallacious objections to Vaccination.

CONTENTS.

PREFACE.

THE following digest of facts may give the public a better notion than it possesses, of what Vaccination is—of what it has done—and of what it can yet do—as a means of saving human life, and lessening human suffering. It is more than probable, the prejudice with which a portion of the public regard the popular medical question—Vaccination—is born rather of ignorance of the real facts of the case, than of a correct knowledge of the subject. Hence, it is a wiser thing to diffuse knowledge freely among the people, so that they may be informed of the grounds on which compulsory legislation on Vaccination is based, than simply to insist on coercion by law, as *the means* by which the benefits of Vaccination are to be extended. The evidence in support of compulsory Vaccination is unquestionably great—indeed so great—that an authority on the subject has declared "that he who disputes it is equally unreasonable as he who opposes in like manner any proposition in Euclid." (*Alison.*) Nevertheless, to compel persons ignorant of such conclusive evidence to obey the law, in the face of the prejudices which they have acquired from fallacious reasoning on what they conceive to be facts, must indeed be worse than useless. How much better is it to appeal to the reason, to supply it with convincing facts bearing on all sides of the subject, than to impose on the transgressors of the law penalties or imprisonment. When these are inflicted, the antipathies (erroneous though they be) against the practice of Vaccination are apt to be thereby incited—and to gain on the public. The would-be-martyrs to the law find no lack of sympathisers,—and thus a strong reaction against the law is encouraged.

Those persons who object to compulsory Vaccination, and exert their influence to move others to oppose it—succeed the best when they dwell almost exclusively on whatever excites the imagination and feelings, so that these may be made to sway the judgment against it. But it is the duty of those who regard Vaccination as a discovery which has conferred—and is still capable of conferring incalculable benefit on the human race, to adopt a different course; they should state in the most distinct manner the *facts* and *reasons* which have led them to decide in favour of Vaccination. The inferences drawn being clearly circumscribed by the facts, the advocates of Vaccination should on this ground alone— on the ground of fact and inference that cannot be disputed—unfold the whole case to the public. In this way, not only the views of opposers of Vaccination may be corrected, but the unsettled opinion of those somewhat doubtful of the benefits of this sanitary measure may be decided.

Those acts of the legislature which deal with health and so-called "personal liberty" should be *supplemented* by the efforts of those who are fully acquainted with the facts and correct inferences from them which have guided the legislature. *Then*—if the law is transgressed, it cannot be wrong to compel obedience. *During epidemics of Small-pox* it is clearly the *duty* of the Guardians of the Public Health, to enforce Vaccination. The State should protect the lives of its subjects when—in times of unusual danger—jeopardised by prejudice or ignorance.

From their scientific education, and Vaccination being part of their daily thought and work, the members of the medical profession ought to constitute the best qualified class to judge correctly of all sides of the question, and to inform the community. They are protectors of health : and inasmuch as life is imperilled by imperfect knowledge and prejudices concerning Vaccination, it is their duty to deal with the arguments urged against this sanitary measure, as much as to prevent disease by any other means. Such a course ought not to be regarded (as it is to be feared it too often is) as undignified.

It is surely a philanthropic work of *any* person convinced of the benefits of Vaccination, to spread a knowledge of the subject—and to meet prejudice and misapprehension with facts.

The public are apt to support the objections commonly urged against Vaccination chiefly because :—

1. They do not possess sufficient knowledge of the subject so as to enable them to decide correctly ; and the facts within their cognizance *often appear* to be in favor of the objections.

2. They are not specially educated in scientific subjects, so as to be enabled to remove sources of fallacy in reasoning ; hence they are apt to allow misinterpretation of facts to sway them against Vaccination.

3. *Personal* experience—even in one or two instances—which appears to tell in favour of the objections, is apt to outweigh all known facts on the other side.   Hence a one-sided view of the question at issue is apt to be taken.

4. The feeling of present security arising from the comparative absence of the evil, (for the removal of which Vaccination was designed) disposes the minds of some to dwell on the *objections to*—rather than on the *benefits of* the remedy.   The experiences of the present are paramount over the recollections of the past, or the probabilities of the future ; the return of the evil, with its former energy and malignity, (when the application of what history has incontestably proved to be the remedy, is relaxed) is apt to be disregarded, because present appearances are fair.   Apparent security encourages a reaction against a practice like Vaccination, which is somewhat inconvenient, and is apt to be regarded as

antiquated and useless. Hence, there is prepared a fitting ground for the rapid growth of prejudice and mis-apprehension.

Though the evidence in favor of Vaccination out-weighs that on the other side, we must not refuse to those who oppose it some credit for sincerity. Misguided though they be in insisting mainly on their objections against this sanitary measure, without giving due weight to the benefits of it, we should not condemn them unheard, or with a high hand, but rather endeavour to sift and test any evidence* they may bring by the store of facts which tell so powerfully against them. It is truth we seek for.

The Vaccination controversy now agitating the public mind, may not be unfruitful of good ; if—in carrying out the practice of Vaccination, increased care is necessary, it will further this desirable result—and the organisation by which Vaccination is applied will be improved by the efforts of those who object rather to it—than to Vaccination itself.

The writer trusts his collection of " Plain Facts on Vaccination," designed as it is for popular use, may help, in however small degree, to advance the good work of diffusing information on the subject through the com-munity.

Redcar, Feb. 1871.

---

* Facts only, not mere *assertions founded on impressions*, can be regarded as evidence.

INTRODUCTORY.

I.—SMALL POX.

THIS is a contagious disease; that is to say, it spreads to the healthy and unprotected from the sick—because these emit from their bodies a contagious or catching poison, apt to seize persons susceptible of its influence. In this respect it resembles Scarlatina, Typhus, Cholera, Measles, Hooping Cough, &c. It belongs to that class of diseases commonly called "Preventable"; because we know of means by which we may reasonably expect to prevent or modify attacks of it, and in this way diminish the mortality. Infectious diseases, regarded by sanitarians as preventable, kill many thousand persons every year, besides carrying into the homes of the community an untold amount of suffering and anxiety. In the ten years from 1856 to 1866, four of these preventable diseases—Small-pox, Scarlatina, Measles, and Hooping-cough—destroyed more than 600,000 of our population; and of these Small-pox alone carried off 60,000 persons. "Such figures as these numerals denote, scarcely convey to the mind an adequate idea of the deplorable loss of life still resulting among us from this one malady. But—to state it otherwise—if in any one year some overwhelming catastrophe destroyed all the living population of the counties of Nairn or Kinross—or swept away every living inhabitant of the cathedral cities of Lichfield, Ripon, or Wells—or slaughtered four or five regiments of soldiers—or smothered as many as five or six times the number of Members of the House of Commons—such an event would assuredly appal and terrify the public and its guardians; and the strongest measures would, no doubt, be called for with the view of preventing the recurrence of the catastrophe, provided its prevention were at all possible. Is the similar amount of human slaughter to which our population is constantly subject by Small-pox—not once, but continuously—not one year, but every year—preventable? I believe that it is so; and I believe further, that the hygienic measures required for effecting this prevention would be found neither specially difficult nor expensive to the country, while they would save annually hundreds, if not thousands, of our population from death by a disease which, even when it spares life, too often leaves permanent lesions, and a broken and damaged constitution."—(*Sir J. Simpson.*) High as is the present mortality from Small-pox, it is insignificant compared with the records of the past ravages

of the disease in the old time before Vaccination was extensively practised; *then* Small-pox produced in Europe the yearly death rate of more than half a million; and it carried off more than 80,000 persons year by year in this kingdom alone. Besides this, it has been estimated that more than *one million* persons every year suffered all the horrible tortures this malignant disease can inflict, and then, escaping with life, were left maimed, blind, deaf, or deeply "pock-holed" and disfigured, carrying with them to the grave traces of the fearful conflict between the disease and life through which they had passed. Now-a-days it is a rare thing to meet with a person blind from Small-pox, or having deep imprints of the disease. The death rate from Small-pox was more than 15 times greater before vaccination than it is now; in other words, for every 15 persons who died from the disease *then* we have but one death *now*. *
This disease alone has in times past destroyed more lives—produced more horrible misery—and more imperilled the prosperity of the human race than the most sanguinary wars and the progress of invading armies. And now, notwithstanding improvements in medical curative science, from 2,000 to 6,000 persons die yearly from Small-pox in this country. This mortality should be still further very much reduced, inasmuch as trustworthy evidence has proved the value and reliability of the

---

* In this country the average annual mortality from Small-pox during 30 years prior to vaccination, was 3,000 for each million of the population; it is now only 202 per million. In Prussia it was 3,422 before vaccination, while now only 276 per million die from Small-pox.

preventive means we possess, and great experience and knowledge have been gained as to the proper use of them.

The contagion of Small-pox has certain well-marked properties :—

1.—It affects the susceptible with almost unerring certainty ; hence Small-pox is, as is well known, the most infectious of all diseases. This fact is best illustrated by tracing the causes of epidemics. The introduction of Small-pox into Leith in 1861 and 1862 is thus described by Sir J. Simpson :—" A beggar woman, on tramp from Newcastle, brought, in the course of her wanderings to Leith, a child lately affected with Small-pox, and with the crusts of the eruption upon it. In Leith she became an inmate of a lodging-house. Many of the lodgers with their children visited the room where the woman and sick child resided. When Dr. Patterson was requested by the magistrates to inspect the tenement, several persons were already dead of Small-pox, caught from this imported case. One man, who had already in previous life suffered from two attacks of Small-pox, visited the infected tenement, and sickened and died of a third attack of the malady. The disease soon spread to other parts of Leith, and 99 human beings were destroyed by it, and much suffering and sickness produced among the many hundreds in the town, who caught the disorder and recovered. The blowing up of the powder magazine in the fort at Leith would not be likely to produce so much danger and destruction of life among the inhabitants of Leith as the advent of the beggar woman and her afflicted child."

2. It undergoes enormous increase and multiplication in the bodies of the affected; an infinitely small quantity of the contagion may set up the disease, and develop in one patient alone, in a few days, a quantity so large that we might infect by it many thousand persons, who, in their turn, might infect many thousands more; for every pustule on the skin is filled with contagion, and the lungs exhale it with every breath. This fact is sufficient to show how far and wide the destructive influence of a person suffering from Small-pox may extend.

3. It affects the *completely unprotected* with great severity, and produces in them a great mortality. Those who have not witnessed a case of malignant Small-pox in the unprotected cannot form a notion of the misery and deformity produced. One such case should cure a whole district prejudiced against Vaccination; and, indeed, it is a notorious fact that prejudice, however inveterate and unmoved by the most powerful appeals to the reason, often melts away before the *presence* of this loathsome disease. As to the mortality, statistics show that one out of three patients dies ; under five years of age one in two ; under two years of age, and about thirty years the proportion which the deaths bear to the recoveries exceeds this; and after sixty hardly any escape.—(*Marson.*)

It is as fatal as Yellow Fever, which kills one in three; more fatal than Typhus, which kills one in five ; and more fatal than Scarlatina, which kills one in ten ; and far more fatal than Cholera was in the epidemics of

1849 and 1854, which affected five millions of the people of the United Kingdom, and produced a mortality of only a quarter of a million, or one in twenty. §

4.   After it has acted upon the system once, it does not as a rule act a second time ; in other words, one attack is a protection against other attacks.   Exceptions to this rule are not very infrequent; but a second attack of Small-pox is certainly *more rare* than a second attack of other infectious diseases.   On this property of the contagion is based the means of protection which have hitherto been resorted to, viz :—

(1.)   *Inoculation* of Small-pox poison into the skin so that it may in that way enter the blood: and

(2.)   *Vaccination* which is the introduction of the contagious matter of Cow-pox through the same channel into the blood.   It is believed by some of the best authorities that Cow-pox itself is merely a remarkably mild form of Small-pox.

II.   INOCULATION OF SMALL POX.

It is a remarkable fact, that when the contagion of Small-pox is introduced into the blood through the skin, a very mild form of the disease almost always follows ; in

§ Dr. Farr in Reports of the Registrar-General.

rare instances only is it severe, or so severe as to resemble the worst cases of Small-pox produced by the *inhalation* of the contagion. This fact was known to the inhabitants of China and Hindostan more than 1,000 years before Christ ; for time out of mind a tribe of Brahmins practised inoculation of Small-pox as a religious cere-mony, and after the operation they invoked the Goddess of Spots for her aid.

The practice of inoculation was not introduced into this country until the early part of the 18th century. In 1841 it became a punishable offence by Act of Parliament, chiefly for these reasons:—

1. It did not reduce the mortality from Small-pox. It was extensively practised in the middle of the 18th century, when Small-pox was very prevalent and fearfully fatal.

2. It spread the poison of Small-pox, so that in every new locality in which it was introduced, it helped in a decided manner to " sow " the disease, because every inoculated person gave off from his body the contagion of Small-pox, which being *inhaled* by the unprotected, produced the ordinary malignant form of the disease. Many epidemics of Small-pox were thus either set up by inoculation, or helped on by it. Thus, at Norwich in 1819, the inoculation of three children with Small-pox was the principal cause of an epidemic of the disease, which destroyed 530 lives in a few months. Epidemics of Small-pox were more frequent while inoculation was practised than they were before, or have been since.

3. The mortality from inoculation was one in 300. *

4. If a second attack of Small-pox occur in the *inoculated* it is not so mild, and it is not attended with so low a mortality as in the *vaccinated*.

5. The same objections as have been urged against Vaccination apply with equal force against inoculation of Small-pox; for instance, if by Vaccination other diseases may be communicated, so they may by inoculation.

But, notwithstanding all these powerful objections to inoculation of Small-pox, there are some circumstances in which it may be justifiable to resort to it; for instance, when Small-pox breaks out among a limited number of persons isolated from the general community, (say on board a ship), when there is no vaccine matter to be got.

* National Vaccine Board.

WHAT IS VACCINATION?

Vaccination is the inoculation into the human system of the infectious matter of a mild disease called Cow-pox. Cow-pox in the cow is regarded by many of our best authorities as in reality Small-pox,* modified and made harmless to the human body by the system of the cow; for it is more apt to affect this animal when Small-pox is epidemic, and it has diminished in exact proportion to the disappearance of Small-pox, so that as a disease it is now almost unknown in the great dairy farms in this country, and finally it has been found that when the cow is inoculated with the contagious matter of malignant Small-pox occurring in man, the animal in consequence suffers from ordinary Cow-pox, and from the disease thus established the human subject may be successfully vaccinated.—(*Simon.*) † A belief in the protective power of Cow-pox over malignant Small-pox prevailed in the

---

* Many authorities, however, believe Cow-pox to be *analogous to*, but *not identical* with Small-pox.

† Horses and sheep have also been affected with a disease like ordinary Cow-pox, and in all probability also a mild form of Small-pox. Monkeys have been affected with epidemics of malignant Small-pox, similar to those which affect the human species, and the

earliest ages in India,* and in those parts of the world, *e.g.* China, &c., which have been affected with Small-pox from time immemorial, as well as in our own country long before the time of Jenner. Benjamin Jesty, a Gloucestershire farmer, in 1774 (22 years before Jenner's first experiment) inoculated with Cow-pox his wife and two sons, for the purpose of protecting them from Small-pox. They were, during 31 years, all frequently exposed to, without catching this disease, and the two sons were *unsuccessfully* inoculated with Small-pox 15 years after the Vaccination. Jesty, when 70 years of age, stated in evidence before the Original Vaccine-Pock Institution, in August, 1805, that ever since he was a boy, now about 60 years ago, it was a *common opinion* where he resided, that persons who had gone through the Cow-pox would not take the Small-pox. He believed he could not take this disease, because he had had Cow-pox. His son, Robert, allowed the Members of the Institute to inoculate him most vigorously for the Small-pox ; and Jesty was vaccinated, *but in neither case with success.* "When the fact became known that he had vaccinated

---

disease has been communicated from these animals to man. Thus, the late Dr. Andrew Anderson observed that a few days before Small-pox appeared in a town called David, in Chirigui, the disease attacked and destroyed many monkeys in the forest. Dying and dead monkeys were seen on the ground covered with the perfect pustules of Small-pox, and several sick monkeys were seen on the trees, moping and moving about in a sickly manner. As to Cow-pox, it has often been observed that persons who feed on the milk of cows affected with this disease remain exempt from genuine Small-pox

*The operation of Vaccination is correctly described in some very ancient Sanscrit writings ; for instance, in a very old Hindoo composition called Sakteya Grantham.

his wife and sons, his friends and neighbours, who had hitherto looked on him with respect, on account of his superior intelligence and honorable character, began to regard him as an inhuman brute, who could dare to practise experiments on his family, the sequel of which would be as they thought—their transformation into horned beasts. Consequently, the worthy farmer was hooted at, reviled, and pelted whenever he attended the markets in his neighbourhood. He remained undaunted, and never failed from this cause to attend to his duties. After living to see another enriched and immortalized for carrying out the same principles for which he had been stoned thirty years before, he died of apoplexy, like Jenner, in 1816."—(*Haviland in Lancet*, 1862.) But it was reserved for Jenner to demonstrate the truth of the vague popular notion by precise scientific experiments. On the 14th of May, 1796, the so-called "birthday of Vaccination," he successfully inoculated Cow-pox from the hand of a milkmaid into the arm of a boy. He thus demonstrated the fact that Cow-pox can be propagated from one person to another. On the 1st of July following the vaccination he inoculated the same boy with Small-pox without effect. In 1801, 6,000 persons had been vaccinated, and the majority of them were inoculated with the poison of malignant Small-pox—but without success. These experiments showed in a most conclusive manner the vaccinated to be proof against Small-pox. Concerning the birthday of Vaccination, M. Lorain truthfully observes "one day he perused in the great book of nature the discovery of Vaccination, and that day he saved from death thousands more than ever fell before a Cæsar or a Napoleon." * To Jenner is due the credit of establishing what is called "arm to arm" Vaccination—of humanizing the contagion of Cow-pox. Vaccination is infinitely superior to inoculation of Small-pox, because it altogether avoids the dangers of this proceeding, and in particular the danger of "sowing" the contagion of Small-pox, for the vaccinated do not give off this contagion from their bodies; and it also protects the system from the malignant disease. In Vaccination a *mild and harmless* form of Small-pox is *voluntarily* accepted in the place of *malignant* Small-pox, which seizes its victims *against their will*.

* Speech in commemoration of Jenner in Paris Faculty of Medicine.

C

WHAT IS MEANT BY BEING "PROPERLY" VACCINATED?

1. Successful Vaccination in early infancy at not fewer than *four* places (six or eight preferable), and :—

2. Successful re-vaccination at *two* places during the period of adolescence *i.e.* from 15 to 20 years of age.

It does not follow because a person has been vaccinated, he has been properly vaccinated, and is in consequence protected (as much as Vaccination can protect) from Small-pox. Hence conclusions relative to Vaccination as a means of shielding the human body from the virulence of malignant Small-pox, and of preventing this disease, drawn from evidence afforded by *all* cases of Vaccination are vitiated by that portion of the evidence furnished by the very numerous class—the imperfectly vaccinated.

I. VACCINATION IN INFANCY.

The best Time for Vaccination.—The law directs that every child shall be vaccinated within the age of 'three calendar months.' To defer the operation beyond this period is unwise, because even under the twelfth month malignant Small-pox is very apt to seize the unprotected and carry them off, and the period of teething (from the 5th to the 24th month) should be avoided.

1. *Small-pox in Infancy and Childhood.*—The Registrar General's returns show that out of every one hundred deaths at all ages from Small-pox,

from 75 to 80 occur within the *fifth year*.

25   ,,   ,,   *twelfth month.*

11   ,,   ,,   *fourth month.*

In other words, *four* out of *five* deaths are those of children under five years of age, an age that should exhibit more exemption from Small-pox than any other, because Vaccination in infancy should be a greater protection to the system *then* than during the remainder of life. But the majority of young children carried off by Small-pox are *unvaccinated* or *very imperfectly* vaccinated. Thus, 80 per cent of the children under three years of age admitted during the latter half of 1870 into the Small-pox Hospital were unvaccinated ; of these 60 per cent died, while not one of the vaccinated children died.—(*Barnes.*) As a practical inference from the foregoing, we may reasonably hope to reduce very considerably the number of deaths from Small-pox by having *every* child vaccinated in *early* infancy. The following facts prove this not an unreasonable position.

Compulsory Vaccination in infancy has been carried out better in Ireland and Scotland than in England or in any other country. In Ireland the annual death-rate from Small-pox was :—

6,000 in 1841

4,000 ,, 1851

1,300 ,, 1861

854   in   1864 (compulsory Act passed)
347   ,,   1865
187   ,,   1866
20   ,,   1867
19*   ,,   1868
nil   ,,   1869—(last quarter,)
1§   ,,   1870—(first quarter.)

In Scotland, where 97 out of every 100 children are vaccinated, the mortality from Small-pox has decreased in like manner. It was—

1054   in   from 1855 to 1865 (yearly average.)
1046   ,,   1863
123   ,,   1866
25   ,,   1870

In no period has the mortality from Small-pox been so small as in the seven years since 1863, when Vaccination was made compulsory.

The only satisfactory explanation of these facts is— Vaccination in infancy, in the first place, by removing the mortality from Small-pox among the unvaccinated during the period of childhood, prevents four out of five deaths and in the second place, the one remaining death is less apt to happen because the contagion of the disease is less diffused through the community.

The risk of death from Small-pox affecting the unvaccinated within the first year of life is very great, inasmuch as statistical returns show that out of each one hundred

* Ten of these were produced by inoculation of Small-pox.
§ *Imported* from the Baltic. A few cases of Small-pox have also been recently *imported* into Belfast and Dublin.

deaths (at all ages) from this disease,

> 25 occur within the *twelfth* month.
>
> 11   ,,   ,,   *fourth* month.

This risk every child runs when Vaccination is delayed beyond the period prescribed by law.

2. *The period of Teething* should be avoided chiefly because :—

(1.) Teething is a source of irritation to the system, and in consequence of it various disorders (in particular eruptions on the skin) are apt to occur. Vaccination likewise sets up irritation and feverishness which may cause disorders similar to those produced by teething. Hence, it would appear to be unwise to resort to Vaccination while teething is going on, if the operation could have been performed safely at an earlier period. But it is even better to vaccinate during the time of teething than to delay the operation until after the expiration of it, because the unprotected child runs a great risk of being seized with, and of dying from Small-pox during the long interval between the 5th and 24th month.

(2.) If the time of teething be not avoided, any skin eruption, and in fact any disorder whatever which may follow Vaccination, and which is common to teething and to Vaccination, may be erroneously attributed to the latter, when in truth it may be the conjoint effect of the two irritations, or merely a harmless result of teething alone.

It may be safely laid down as a general rule that Vaccination should be performed *between the sixth and twelfth week from birth,* and should not be delayed beyond this period, unless ill-health postpones the operation.

THE NUMBER AND CHARACTER OF THE MARKS
OR SCARS LEFT BY VACCINATION.

1. *Number of Marks.*—Mr. Marson, of the Small-pox Hospital, has shown *the mortality from Small-pox after Vaccination varies with the number of marks.* His observations are based on 15,000 cases.   He found that in every 100 cases of Small-pox after Vaccination having

1 mark 8 died (7·73)

2 ,, 5 ,, (4·7)

3 ,, 2 ,, (1·95)

and in every 200 with four or more marks only one died.

The same observer showed that out of 100 *unvaccinated* cases 35 died. * In other words, the chances of recovery from Small-pox are—

as 200 to 1 in persons having 4 marks of Vaccination

,, 100 to 2 ,,   ,, 3 ,,   ,,

,, 100 to 5 ,,   ,, 2 ,,   ,,

,, 100 to 8 ,,   ,, 1 ,,   ,,

but only 100 to 35 ,,   non-vaccinated.

From this evidence it would appear to be proved that to secure in the highest degree the protective power of Vaccination, the contagious matter of Cow-pox should be introduced in not fewer than *four* places.

2. *Character of the Scars.*—Each scar should be distinctly covered all over with little pits, like the end of a thimble.‡   Mr. Marson has shown that out of one hundred

---

* "The death-rate from Small-pox at the London Small-pox Hospital for 51 years, was 35 per cent. among the unvaccinated."—(*Seaton.*)

‡ "Vaccination may be relied on when four or more vesicles have formed which have left good dotted cicatrices (Scars.)—*Marson.*

cases of Small-pox prevented by Vaccination having—

11 good scars 3 died (2·52)

21 very imperfect scars 9 died (8·82)

II.   RE-VACCINATION.

This important subject is considered in the next chapter.

IS RE-VACCINATION NECESSARY ?

About nineteen years after the introduction of Vaccination it was observed the vaccinated occasionally took a mild form of Small-pox.   The experience of more than half a century has proved the protection afforded by Vaccination in infancy is not life-long—it is only temporary.   The following facts show that an attack of *Small-pox* may only prove to be this, we cannot expect Vaccination to be more.   Of (in round numbers) 6,000 boys admitted into the Royal Military Asylum,

2,000 had scars of Small-pox,

4,000   ,,   Vaccination.

Small-pox affected *both classes nearly in the same propor-tion, i. e.* about six in each 1,000.

When re-vaccination is *successful* it is presumed previous Vaccination has lost its influence, and exposure to infection (especially when Small-pox is epidemic) may induce an attack ; when *unsuccessful* it is believed Vaccination in infancy holds good : should Small-pox occur it will be mild, and the mortality almost *nil*.   Inasmuch as *re-vac-cination is not general*, it would appear from the following facts the number of persons completely protected by Vaccination in infancy only must be small ; and conversely that *the imperfectly protected form a very large class.*

Three hundred and seventy-six children (ages varying from eight to fifteen years), were recently re-vaccinated by Messrs. Alford and Gervis, at the Orphan Working School, Haverstock Hill; in 321 (or 85 per cent) the operation was successful. Dr. Barnes in 1861 successfully re-vaccinated 82 out of 95 children.

Our Army Medical Reports show that out of every 100 soldiers—re-vaccination was successful in

> 64 having *good marks* of Vaccination.
>
> 72   ,,   *imperfect marks*   ,,
>
> 81   *not having marks*   ,,

In other words, from 64 to 72 per cent. of the vaccinated, and 81 per cent of the unvaccinated, would in all probability, had they been exposed to the infection, *have taken Small-pox but for re-vaccination.* The same reports show that re-vaccination was successful in 59 per cent of those who had had *Small-pox.* In the Prussian army 63 per cent. of the re-vaccinations performed during the 36 years from 1833 to 1869, have been successful.

The value of re-vaccination is further shown by the following facts :—

In the Army of Würtemberg the infection of Small-pox was introduced sixteen times in the five years, from 1833 to 1837. Among the 14,384 re-vaccinated soldiers,—only one single instance of *modified* Small-pox occurred.—(*Heim.*)

In the Prussian Army re-vaccination has been practised since 1833. Nearly two millions of soldiers have been re-accinated. The annual number of deaths from Small-pox in this immense army from 1833 to 1867 is slightly over 3—while it was 104 before 1833 ; in other words, the practice of re-vaccination has in this instance reduced the annual mortality from Small-pox from 104 to 3.   In the 20 years following the adoption of re-vaccination there were only 40 deaths from Small-pox, (2 deaths per annum), and *only 4 of these had been re-vaccinated successfully.* In 1866 there were 14 cases of Small-pox, of these

    1 had been re-vaccinated *without success.*

    13 *had not been re-vaccinated.*

In 1867 *none of the cases of Small-pox* had been *re-vaccinated.*   These facts are taken at random from the returns of the Prussian Army.   They are supported by similar evidence in the Swedish, Danish, and British Armies and the Army of Baden.

Heim observes that among 30,000 *re-vaccinated* persons in civil practice, there were, within five consecutive years, only *two cases* * of *modified* Small-pox ; while, within the same period, there were 1,674 cases among a population o 363,225 persons not vaccinated and not re-vaccinated. The proportion which the number of attacks bore to the population was, therefore, in the two classes :—

    Re-vaccinated 1 in 15,000.

    Not re-vaccinated 1 in 217.

Inasmuch as if the 30,000 re-vaccinated persons had suffered alike with the others, there would have been among them 138 cases instead of 2, it may be presumed that re-vaccination prevented 136 seizures of Small-pox.

---

* It was uncertain whether one of these cases was not Chicken-pox.

" The nurses and servants at the Small-pox Hospital, when they enter the service, are invariably submitted to Vaccination, which in their case generally is re-vaccination, and is never afterwards repeated ; and so perfect is the protection, that though nurses live in the closest and most constant attendance on Small-pox patients, and though, also, the other servants are in various ways exposed to special chances of infection, the Resident Surgeon of the Hospital, during his thirty-four years of office there, has *never known Small-pox affect any one of these nurses or servants."* (*Memorandum of Medical Department of the Privy Council*). When the Small-pox Hospital was built, many of the workmen were employed about the building and wards for several months after the arrival of patients ; the majority were re-vaccinated, and *not a single case of Small-pox* occurred among them ; but there were *two cases* among the few who *objected to re-vaccination.*

Medical men rely on the protection afforded by re-vaccination, and they very rarely take Small-pox. During the epidemic in Paris, the re-vaccinated physicians and attendants on the sick have hitherto escaped the dreadful scourge which has carried off many thousands of the unprotected.

Epidemics of Small-pox can be speedily arrested by re-vaccination. In France the disease has thus been extinguished in the Army Corps, especially in the *Garde-de-Paris* and in various public and private establishments. ' A few weeks ago St. George's Hospital seemed a hot-bed for the disease, and a centre of infection for the locality; yet, by promptly stopping all visitors, by isola-

tion of the sick, and by *re-vaccinating* all belonging to
the Hospital, the spread of the malady was speedily and
completely arrested." (*Medical Times and Gazette, Feb.*
11*th*, 1871) The influence of re-vaccination on the progress of epidemics of Small-pox is well shown by the following remarks by DR. GINTRAC in the *Gazette des Hopi-
taux*, 11*th July*, 1857 :—

"In a parish containing a population of about 2,600
souls, a young woman who had been vaccinated was attacked towards the end of October, 1853, with Small-
pox contracted during a long residence with a relation
suffering from that disease. During the whole of her
illness this young woman was attended by her mother,
who also took the disease, although she was fifty-seven
years of age, and had been vaccinated. Both recovered :
but, early in January, at the beginning of her mother's
convalescence, the disease became epidemic. It invaded
families, attacking each member in succession or simul-
taneously. In January, the number of persons seized ex-
ceeded 180, and by the 10th of February it had reached
nearly 260. From day to day the number rapidly increased.
There were *no cases* of Small-pox in *vaccinated* subjects
under twelve years of age. The *greater the age of those
attacked*, or in other words, *the longer the interval since
Vaccination, the greater was the severity of the disease.*
Some families strikingly exemplified the remarkable relation which existed between the more or less advanced
age of the patient, and the greater or less severity of the
attack. In a family of eight, (father, mother and six

children), the parents had confluent (the worst form of) Small-pox; three sons, aged 26, 23, and 22 respectively, had the disease less severely; two sons, aged 18 and 15, had modified Small-pox; and the other son, aged 12, though constantly exposed to the contagion in the same room with the others, had no eruption at all. It was ascertained that in general, the disease was decidedly modified, and essentially milder, in those who had been vaccinated: in them the duration of the attack was less than half of the usual duration. There were no fatal cases among the patients who had been vaccinated. Ten deaths occurred among the unvaccinated. In February, 1854, in less than ten days, 180 Vaccinations and 712 re-vaccinations were performed. The result surpassed the most sanguine hopes. The persons who had been vaccinated and re-vaccinated successfully or unsuccessfully, almost all escaped Small-pox. There were five exceptions, but in these cases, Vaccination only preceded the eruption of Small-pox by a few days. The following are some of the conclusions drawn from the observations made during the epidemic.

" Small-pox did not attack indiscriminately and by chance: it generally seized the old, and respected the young. If this epidemic has shown that Cow-pox is not absolutely preservative, it has at least established that it exerts a salutary influence upon the issue of an attack of Small-pox by shortening its duration and lessening its danger.

"Re-vaccination applied generally to a population during

the full tide of an epidemic has at once arrested its ravages and destroyed its power of development. Finally, re-vaccination performed in the midst of an epidemic has been found to be free from all bad consequences, notwithstanding the fears of evil which were entertained by some physicians."

These facts prove that in order to continue the protection afforded by Vaccination in infancy beyond the period of childhood and youth re-vaccination is necessary.

The best authorities are of opinion that Vaccination properly performed in infancy will as a rule protect the system until the age of puberty; they therefore direct that re-vaccination should be performed some time between the fifteenth and twentieth year, and they regard persons vaccinated in infancy and at the sixteenth year as permanently protected. —(*Ballard.*) " The practice of *repeated* or periodic re-vaccination does not appear to be generally necessary. But in instances where a person, after re-vaccination has been subjected to serious constitutional or climatic changes, and is subsequently more than ordinarily exposed to the infection of Small-pox a *further* re-vaccination may properly be advised."—(*Royal College of Physicians*, 1871.)

It cannot be too much insisted on that re-vaccination is *as necessary* as primary Vaccination. Every person, on attaining the age of 16 years, should be re-vaccinated *whether Small-pox be prevalent or not*. It is unwise to wait for the terrible warning of approaching Small-pox because then a ' Vaccination panic' is apt to arise, and medical men are often unable to meet the enormously in-creased demand for fresh healthy lymph, when delay is more than usually dangerous. In this way the march of the enemy is encouraged, for it seizes almost exclusively the *un-vaccinated*, the *imperfectly vaccinated*, and those *who have not had the ordinary forethought of undergoing the simple operation of re-vaccination* in times of appa-rent security.

When Small-pox is epidemic, children (irrespective of age) and adults should be re-vaccinated. *Without re-vac-cination no person is safe from catching the disease.*

Inasmuch as the re-vaccinated *generally* fail to afford a supply of lymph for Vaccination, parents and other *non-re-vaccinated* members of a household should be re-vaccinated when a healthy child belonging to it is successfully vac-cinated. *Systematic* re-vaccination would then become *the rule* at all times, rather than as it is now—*the ex-ception.*

Persons who have had Small-pox should be re-vaccinated because if they become again susceptible to the contagion of Small-pox, the harmless operation of Vaccination may save them from a second attack.

If, in any case re-vaccination is *unsuccessful* it should be repeated at stated intervals, for instance every year, and whenever Small-pox appears in the house or neighbourhood, *until it is successful,* because *the system may become sus-ceptible to Small-pox some time after unsuccessful attempts at re-vaccination.*

DOES VACCINATION PROTECT FROM SMALL POX?

1. Dr. Jenner and others inoculated many thousands of vaccinated persons with the poison of Small-pox without producing this disease.

Drs. Buchanan and Seaton on inspecting 50,000 children in various charities and National Schools, found the numbers having marks of Small-pox in the two classes—vaccinated and un-vaccinated, as follow :—

1. *Children with marks of Vaccination.*

   *2 in each 1,000 had scars of Small-pox.

2. *Children with no marks of Vaccination.*

   360 out of each 1000 had scars of Small-pox.

From these figures we may infer that in 358 children out of each 1,000 Vaccination proved a protective against Small-pox.

3. Number of deaths from Small-pox out of every 1,000 deaths from all causes during :—

---

* Correctly 1.78.

50 years before Vaccination—50 years after Vaccination
        (of *last* century.) ...   (of *this* century.)

England	96	...	...	35
German States	66	...	...	7
	1660—1679	...	...	1859
London	36	...	...	4*

4. Small-pox is least fatal when Vaccination is properly carried out,—and conversely. The following is the mortality from Small-pox in each 1000 deaths from all causes—in countries where

(1.) *Vaccination is voluntary and neglected.*

England and Wales	...	22
Ireland	...	49†

(2.) *Vaccination is compulsory.*

Sweden ...	...	3
Lombardy ...	...	2
Bohemia ...	...	2
Bavaria ...	...	4
Austria ...	...	6
Rhenish Provinces	...	4
Saxony ...	...	8
Westphalia ...	...	6

In Denmark Vaccination was made compulsory in 1810. During the 12 preceding years 3,000 persons died from Small-pox in Copenhagen alone, but for the 15 following years the disease entirely disappeared.

" Wherever Vaccination falls into neglect, Small-pox tends to become again the same frightful pestilence it

---

* Returns of Registrar-General.
† *Before* the death rate of Small-pox was diminished by efficient Vaccination.

was in the days before Jenner's discovery; wherever Vaccination is universally and properly performed, Small-pox tends to be of as little effect as any extinct epidemic of the middle ages."—(*Simon.*)

5. The vaccinated residing in communities unprotected from Small-pox almost always escape, while many thousands of the un-vaccinated perish.

During the twenty years, from 1818 to 1838,

(1.) In the West Indies, many thousands of the native population were carried off by Small-pox,—-but among the vaccinated troops stationed there (121,000) there were *no deaths* from it, and among the vaccinated black troops there was not *one* case of it.

(2.) In Western Africa, the vaccinated white troops wholly escaped, while the black unprotected population died by hundreds from malignant Small-pox.

(3.) In Malta, there were only *two deaths* from Small-pox in the troops (40,826) while in the year 1830 alone, 1.048 of the population died.

Proportion of attacks.				Died.
Natives ... 1 in 12 ...	...	...	...	1 in 85.
Military ... 1 ,, 118 ...	...	...	...	1 ,, 682.

(Including wives and children.)

(4.) In Ceylon, 3,208 of the natives died out of 9,105 attacked, while only 14 of the Military died, and in the epidemic of 1834 there was not one case among the soldiers.

6. History shows that Small-pox introduced into a community wholly unprotected is apt to produce a fearful

loss of life. "In 1520, a negro covered with pustules of Small-pox was landed on the Mexican coast. From him the disease spread with such desolation, that within a very short time, 3½ millions of people were destroyed in Mexico alone." "Small-pox was introduced into Iceland in 1707, when 16,000 persons were carried off by its ravages:—more than a fourth part of the whole population of the island." "It reached Greenland in 1733, and spread so fatally as almost to depopulate the country."—(*Sir Thos. Watson.*)

7. *The effect of Vaccination on epidemics of Small-pox.*—Since Vaccination has been practised the number of epidemics has diminished.

In this country, in 100 years, there were,

    Before *Inoculation* of Small-pox 71 epidemics ;
    During   ,,   ,,   84   ,,
    ,, *Vaccination*   ,,   24   ,,

Epidemics of Small-pox never occur in our Army and Navy, nor in the properly vaccinated soldiers and seamen of other countries.—(*Aitken.*)

SMALL-POX IN THE VACCINATED:

WHAT INFLUENCE DOES VACCINATION EXERT ON THE ATTACK, AND ON THE MORTALITY?

As a rule Cow-pox is a perfect or permanent protection against Small-pox; exceptions, however, are numerous. The properly vaccinated, not unfrequently catch Small-pox, and, in rare instances, die from it.

1. *The nature of the attack.* Small-pox when it seizes the vaccinated is disarmed of its malignity. The attack as a rule is so mild and modified as to be regarded as a distinct form of the disease. Hence Vaccination is often resorted to,—*even after the unprotected have been exposed to the contagion of Small-pox*—not so much for preventing attacks of this disease, as for divesting them of their severity.

2. *The mortality.* According to Mr. Marson's statistics in each 100 unvaccinated cases 35 died.

      ,,   200 properly vaccinated 1 died.

      ,,   100 cases vaccinated with various degrees of efficiency 5 died.

Of 400 deaths at the Small-pox Hospital, only 3 were

properly vaccinated, over 100 were unvaccinated, and the remainder were imperfectly vaccinated.*

During the epidemic now raging in London, of 433 cases admitted into the Small-pox Hospital, Hampstead— 316 had been vaccinated, and 117 unvaccinated; the mortality of the former was only 5 per cent.—that of the latter 41 per cent., or *eight* times greater. While the chances of recovery among the vaccinated are 20 to 1, in severe epidemics they are nearly 2 to 1 among the un-vaccinated. Inasmuch as the unvaccinated form a com-paratively *small* class (estimated at from 1 to 2 in 10) so *large* a proportionate mortality among them is a sig-nificant fact; and the relatively *small* mortality among the properly vaccinated, illustrates in a striking manner the benign influence of Vaccination. Besides this, it would appear to be shown by the following facts that Vaccination is even a better protection from death than a previous attack of Small-pox itself. At the Royal Military Asylum, 28 vaccinated boys took Small-pox, and none died; 12 boys who had scars of Small-pox on admission took the disease, and 4 died: a mortality of 33 per cent.—nearly the death rate of the unvaccinated.

Mr. Marson has shown that of each 100 cases having previously had Small-pox, 19 died—a death rate nearly *four* times greater than that of the vaccinated.

---

*The following table shows the percentage of deaths in the two classes—vaccinated and non-vaccinated—at the Small-pox Hospital each year from 1863 to 1867 (inclusive):

	1863.	1864.	1865.	1866.	1867.
Non-vaccinated	48	36	38	35·7	36·8
Vaccinated	12	8·7	7·4	7·3	8·29

DOES THE PRACTICE OF VACCINATION ACCOUNT FOR THE REMARKABLE DIMINUTION OF SMALL-POX IN VACCINATED COMMUNITIES?

Those who oppose Vaccination are wont to ascribe the disappearance of Small-pox to : —

1. Improved sanitary condition of vaccinated communities.

2. The tendency which epidemics have to gradually die out.

The following evidence disproves this opinion.

1. Small-pox is as prevalent and fatal in countries where Vaccination is unknown, or is imperfectly practised, as it was in this kingdom before the time of Jenner. Japan and India àre examples. Dr. Pringle thus describes Small-pox in India.

" I would beg to add that, after a continuous residence of nearly 13 years in India, and having seen Cholera in its most fatal haunts during three years at Juggernaut, and witnessed the effects of famine, I have arrived at the conclusion that, though the former may count its victims by hundreds, and the latter by larger numbers though at longer periods, yet both pale before the spectre of Small-pox, stalking yearly through densely crowded villages, and seizing its victims from the children born since its last visit, with a mortality which it is appalling to contemplate; and knowing this as I do, I confess to feeling an earnest desire to do all that in me lies to check a scourge allowed to be preventable. If during my short stay in this country I have succeeded in enlisting on the side of Vaccination one tithe of the sympathy and help which the subject demands, I feel I shall not have pleaded in vain for the infant population of Hindostan."

" So fatal is Small-pox among children, that the following has become quite a saying among the agricultural, and, indeed, the wealthiest classes, viz, ' Never to count children as permanent members of the family, nor to leave them money or make any arrangements for their future, *until* they have been attacked with and recovered from Small-pox.' "

The sanitary condition is much the same in all parts of India. Nevertheless, in some districts where Vaccination is well carried out, Small-pox has greatly diminished. Thus at Rhutpore, Dr. Harvey reports the disease " almost stamped out by efficient Vaccination." In districts where the population is unvaccinated, or even imperfectly Vaccinated, the disease rages with fearful fatality. Thus of the district of Rajpootana, Surgeon Moore writes, "Small-pox is indeed now in this locality more destructive than Cholera or any other malady; what Macaulay wrote of England before the days of Jenner is now applicable here."

2. In districts of Great Britain where the sanitary condition is unsatisfactory, Small-pox has declined in direct proportion to the application of careful Vaccination, thus it has been almost banished from Ireland and Scotland. During past epidemics the Union of Poplar suffered severely through neglected Vaccination ; in it there were

> 97 deaths from Small-pox in 1863.
> 66   ,,   ,,   ,,   1866.
> 112   ,,   ,,   ,,   1867.

But only 11   ,,   ,,   ,,   1870, because, since 1868, special attention has been paid to Vaccination. This reduction of mortality cannot be explained by improvement of the sanitary condition.

The Holborn Union (including the unsanitary districts of Holborn, Clerkenwell, and St. Pancras) has also had a low death-rate from Small-pox since Vaccination was properly attended to, while in adjoining imperfectly vaccinated districts, Small-pox has raged with great fatality.

"In the City of London Union the disease has been stamped out by Vaccination."*

In the district of Pinchbeck, Lincolnshire, (population 3,000), for many years under the medical charge of Mr. T. Stiles, (who twice received the Government grant for efficient Vaccination) there has only been *one*

---

* Asserted by Mr. Sutor, a City Guardian

death from Small-pox during the last thirty years, viz. a young man who had never been vaccinated. (*Lancet.*)

The population is apt to suffer from Small-pox *in porportion to the neglect of Vaccination,* irrespective of any conditions affecting the Public Health. This is illustrated by the case of Denmark, where Small-pox disappeared entirely for fifteen years, and then returned because of the neglect of Vaccination engendered by the absence of the scourge.

In France, general neglect of Vaccination for many years past, by allowing an accumulation of unprotected persons, prepared the way for the present epidemic ; and the enormous mortality from Small-pox during the siege is in great part accounted for by thousands of unvaccinated and imperfectly vaccinated persons having fled to Paris from the provinces before the siege commenced.—(*Seaton.*)

During 1870 more than *one-half* of the mortality (281) in the Eastern districts of London occured in two Unions —Bethnal-Green and Mile-End old Town,—the Guardians of which, being opposed to Vaccination, have not carried out the provisions of the compulsory Vaccination Act. (*Seaton.*)

3. Irrespective of improvements in sanitary affairs since the last century, the mortality from Small-pox (over 30 per cent.) among the un-vaccinated remains the same. At Newcastle-upon-Tyne during 1864-68 the mortality of the never-vaccinated was 37 per cent., of the vaccinated 2 per cent., or 19 times less.—(*Philipson.*)

The death rate of the unvaccinated at the Small-pox

Hospital during the epidemic year, 1863, was 47 per cent, and in the present epidemic it is 41 per cent.

4. In Public Institutions, such as Small-pox Hospitals, the patients, vaccinated and unvaccinated, are in exactly similar circumstances, yet the mortality among them is remarkably different, a fact which can only be explained by the benign influence of Vaccination.

Epidemic diseases are apt to rage during a long series of years with fearful violence, and then gradually subside. It is believed by some that Small-pox, being an example of this law, was on the wane, its virulence exhausted, when Vaccination was introduced. This opinion is disproved by these considerations.

1. A worn out epidemic is less malignant; Small-pox is still as fatal among the never-vaccinated as in former times. Like other infectious diseases, Small-pox may in some epidemics carry off a large proportion of those attacked, while in others it may produce a comparatively low mortality. Hence, opposers of Vaccination *can easily select mild epidemics in times past*, to show how much the death-rate from Small-pox before Vaccination, is exaggerated; but such partial conclusions must be corrected by other statistics indicating a higher mortality than the estimated average, and by the death rate of the un-vaccinated in Public Institutions.

2. The disease is clearly not disposed to die out, because wherever Vaccination is neglected it is to apt to break forth with its pristine energy and fatality.

3. It is controlled by Vaccination *now* wherever, as in

India, it is still a scourge, as it was in this country before Vaccination was practised.

Although because of Vaccination, Small-pox is the most preventable of infectious diseases, observance of sanitary precautions is none the less necessary, because it may arrest the development of the contagion, and thus the un-vaccinated, and even the vaccinated, run less risk of catching it;—of these precautions the most important are *(a)* DISINFECTION, and *(b)* ISOLATION of the sick from the healthy. During the Parisian epidemic, cases of Small-pox and patients suffering from other diseases, were treated together in the same hospital wards :—there being no Small-pox Hospitals in Paris. The rapid extension of the epidemic is attributed to want of isolation, as well as neglect of Vaccination.

OBJECTIONS COMMONLY URGED AGAINST VACCINATION.

The accusations brought against Vaccination arraigned at the bar of *public opinion* should be supported or disproved by observation and fact.

While on the one hand, the modifying influence of Vaccination on malignant Small-pox may be admitted, on the other, it may be contended its injurious effects on those who have undergone the operation outweigh the evils of uncontrolled Small-pox, or the modification of this disease is counterbalanced by the encouragement of others, so that the amount of disease and death is un-altered. Such defined questions may be fairly dealt with, —beset though the discussion is by numerous sources of fallacious inference. Objections against Vaccination arising from mere *impressions* or *antipathies*, without foundation on fact and reasoning, cannot be discussed in this way. They must be corrected by the imparting of information. Objections to Vaccination are commonly urged on the following grounds :—

(1) Local effects.
(2) Constitutional effects.
(3) The reduction of Small-pox by Vaccination counterbalanced by the substitution or extension of other diseases.
(4) The inferiority of the ordinary mode of Vaccination compared with Vaccination from the Cow.

I.—THE LOCAL EFFECTS OF VACCINATION.

Cow-pox, like other infectious disorders, is attended with local irritation. Round the vaccine spots are signs of slight inflammation,—redness, swelling, and tenderness. This harmless inflammation, aggravated by certain causes, is apt to produce the "bad arm." The vaccinated part may then swell considerably—the inflammatory blush spread to adjoining parts—the vaccine spots ulcerate, and an abscess even form in the arm-pit from simple irritation, just as the irritating constriction of a tight boot may lead to abscess in the groin; or, in rare cases, genuine erysipelas may arise in the irritated part, and invade the structures around.

When the local effects of Vaccination are severe, and especially when they last some time, and produce simple eruptions on distant parts of the body, it is a common error to ascribe them to contamination of the blood by Vaccination. Before we can correctly draw such a conclusion, other causes should be excluded.

IRRITATION OF THE VACCINATED PART BY

(1) *Tight Clothing.*—The least movement of the

vaccinated arm constricted by dress is apt (particularly about the eighth day of Vaccination) to increase the usual irritation of the vaccine punctures. Thus even a hard irritable ulcer leading to abscess may be produced. These effects more frequently follow re-vaccination than Vaccination in infancy. Irritation should be reduced as much as possible by keeping the vaccinated arm at rest and free from pressure.

(2) *Irritating Clothing.*—Woollen and cotton are apt to irritate a wound however slight, and should be avoided. A piece of linen smeared with simple ointment, or sweet olive oil is the best covering.

(3) *Scratching* of the vaccinated part may set up much inflammation.

(4.) *Poisoning of the vaccine punctures by substances undergoing decomposition.*—The vaccine punctures and the blood may be poisoned by accidental contact with dirt or foreign matter: by this means fatal erysipelas has been induced. This disease, more liable to occur from any slight irritation (even in children apparently healthy) when Vaccination is at its height, than at other times, may be set up in this simple way :—A mother or nurse may accidentally have her dress touched (say by soiled fingers) with fish or any other substance apt to undergo *rapid decomposition*, and while nursing, the vaccinated part by being brought into contact with the smeared surface, is poisoned.

Death from want of cleanliness is *not* death from Vaccination. The popular prejudice against the bathing and washing of infants under Vaccination is erroneous ; if necessary, the vaccinated part may be washed *immediately* after the operation without affecting the result, because the lymph enters the blood almost *instantaneously* —once there, no amount of washing can remove it. *

HEALTH OF THE VACCINATED CHILD.

A weakly unhealthy child, or even a child apparently robust, though recognised by medical men as scrofulous, or in constitution otherwise affected, is very apt to suffer more than usual from the local effects of Vaccination, notwithstanding the greatest care in avoiding irritation of the vaccinated part. In such children, *any local inflammation*, however innocent, is *peculiarly liable to run a troublesome course.* This source of fallacy in reading correctly the causes of the more severe local results of Vaccination is not understood by those not devoted to the study of disease, and the hidden influences of constitutional disorders. *Ill-health* of the vaccinated is a *predisposing cause* of erysipelas. In Children's Hospitals a fatal form of this disease after Vaccination of the patients is not very uncommon,—(*Trousseau and Giraldes*)—yet this experience does not form a reason

---

* This fact has been proved by experiment. In 1863, Dr. Peter, of Paris, vaccinated 60 infants on both arms. *Immediately* after the operation he washed one arm of each child, and rubbed it vigorously. The vesicles of Cow-pox developed on *both* arms, but were more numerous and beautiful on the washed arm.

In 1862 Dr. Martin *cauterized* the punctures of Vaccination a *few minutes* after he made them. The absorption of the lymph was not prevented, because in the subject so treated all subsequent attempts to produce Cow-pox were ineffectual.—*(Trousseau.)*

or abstaining from the Vaccination of sickly children *during an epidemic of Small-pox*, inasmuch as almost every infant or weakly child taking this disease dies. Erysipelas, precisely similar to that which may follow Vaccination, not unfrequently affects children who have never been vaccinated. The following, related by Dr. Woodward, of Worcester, is an example;—"I was requested to visit the infant child of Mrs Heath, residing at Perry Wood, (who has given me permission to publish the case). It was in a dangerous state, from severe erysipelatous inflammation of the left arm, extending from the shoulder to the elbow. It was exactly similar in appearance to what I have seen in one or two other cases *after* Vaccination, and on my remarking that I supposed if the child had been lately vaccinated the illness would have been attributed to that cause, she said it certainly would, and that 'nothing (to use her own words) would have made her believe the contrary,' and at which I certainly could not be surprised. Fortunately in this case the parents had been opposed to Vaccination, having four or five children all unvaccinated. I afterwards vaccinated the whole of them, including the infant after its recovery—they all did well, and one of the children was declared to have been benefitted in its health by Vaccination. Now had this infant chanced to have been vaccinated just before its illness, (which might easily have happened), and this had terminated fatally, very possibly a similar request would have been made to one which appeared some time ago, viz., to have

the words '*died from the mortal effects of Vaccination*'
inscribed on the tombstone ; as such deaths are so
singular, it is a pity that it was not recorded in that
manner, and the wish of the individual thus gratified."

II.—THE CONSTITUTIONAL EFFECTS OF VACCINATION.

Signs of constitutional disorder appearing after Vaccination are often ascribed to the so-called poisoning or con-
taminating influence of this operation. As they may arise
from other causes, we should, in order to avoid false inferences, exclude them before we can with justice charge Vaccination. Two very obvious facts succeed one another—
Vaccination, and a skin, or other disorder ; the public are
apt to connect them as cause and effect, because *they are
consecutive*, and as a rule *the only facts known* from which
an inference may be drawn. Hence *any disorder whatever*
occuring shortly after Vaccination is apt to be attributed to
this operation.

The less obvious, *though powerful* causes of disease in
infancy are mostly unknown to the public, or to persons
untutored in medical science and reasoning ; hence, they
may easily draw incorrect conclusions concerning the supposed injurious effects of Vaccination.

The diseases said to be peculiarly liable to conveyance
by Vaccination are :—

(1) Scrofula and Consumption.

(2) Skin affections.

I.—SCROFULA AND CONSUMPTION.

These constitutional disorders may exist with apparent
health ;—when constitutional and *undeveloped* they may not

E

betray to *ordinary observation* local indications of their presence, while as a rule, they are easily recognised by medical men.
*They do not endanger life unless they settle in some impor-
tant organ*, such as the lungs.   This local development is
favoured by any cause which may *weaken* the system ; for
example, fevers, and especially eruptive fevers, such as
Small-pox.   Medical authorities regard Small-pox as more
powerful than any other disease as an *exciting* cause of the
local manifestations of Scrofula.   Hence, when this disease
prevailed extensively, as during the last century, the mortality from Scrofula and Consumption was very great.
" During the middle of the last century, before Vaccination
was known, the Scrofulous death-rate was *more than five
times as great* as our present one ; and the pulmonary
[consumptive] death-rate of the present time is 7 *per cent.
lower* than that of 1746-55."—(*Greenhow.*)   Dr. Farr has
also worked out the same results from separate data.
Inasmuch as this evidence proves Small-pox to have *developed* Scrofulous disorders more powerfully than have Cow-
pox, or other infectious diseases, if the controlling influence of Vaccination over the virulence or prevalence of
Small-pox be admitted, it will follow that it has *diminished*
rather than (as alleged) increased the mortality from Scrofula and Consumption.   The only inference compatible with
these facts is, that Vaccination either does not develop these
diseases, or it does so to an *infinitely smaller degree* than
Small-pox; and if it be allowed that it *may spread a constitutional taint,* the ordinary causes of debility would develop
it ;—and as the local diseases thus induced are known to

be peculiarly fatal, there *should* be an increased mortality from them.

II.— SKIN DISEASES.

These disorders after Vaccination may be due to:—

1.   *Teething.*—Vaccination is usually performed shortly before teething, which is known to be a very prolific cause of skin diseases in infancy.

2.   *Irritation of Stomach and Bowels from improper feeding.*   Much ignorance prevails respecting infant-feeding. Hence, disorders of the digestive organs are common, and they often produce eruptions on the skin.

The following case reported by Dr. A. Farr, shows how an apparently alarming skin affection, wrongly attributed to Vaccination, may arise from an obscure cause operating through the food :— a cause which would elude detection by any but those educated in medical reasoning.

" On Wednesday last, a child at the breast, which, on the previous Thursday, had been vaccinated at the Surrey Chapel Station, Blackfriars-road, by Mr. Marson, was brought to me covered by an eruption *(urticaria)* which the mother and her neighbours declared was caused by the Vaccination. The state of the child with swollen face, with the breathing hurried and difficult, and the bloated condition of its body generally, at first somewhat puzzled me, and I was disposed to believe that it was a harmless rash produced by irritation, but the state of the arm not warranting such a belief, and it suddenly occurring to me that the symptoms were so strikingly like those resulting from fish poisoning, I was led to ask the mother if it was at all probable that she had been eating stale fish, when I learned that on the night previous to the eruption making its appearance she had taken mussels to supper. Being now satisfied that the mischief *had been communicated through the breast,* I treated the case as one of ordinary nettle-rash. The next morning there was comparatively little eruption to be seen."

3. *Constitutional peculiarity of the vaccinated child.*— When the skin is delicate and irritable, Cow-pox like any *simple* irritant may induce a harmless though troublesome rash on various parts of the body.

Scrofulous children are more liable than others to extensive eruptions and sores after Vaccination, notwithstanding the most careful selection of lymph. In such cases Vaccination like any other irritation, * — however harmless — may, in rare cases, excite the development of Scrofula on the skin. The scrofulous constitution is hereditary; hence, *several members of the same family* may have obstinate skin affections from this cause after Vaccination. So *many* apparent examples of the injurious effects of this operation occurring *together*, are apt to encourage opposition to the practice of Vaccination. Constitutional diseases very often exist in the families of those who oppose Vaccination : their objections or doubts respecting it spring from personal experience of what *appears to be communication of diseases by Vaccination ;* but the maladies thus set up, when read aright by the light

---

* *e.g.* a blister, or the simple operation of piercing the ears: these simple irritants have sometimes set up obstinate eruptions in scrofulous children.

of medical science, prove to be merely the local developments of latent disorders of the system, *ready to appear* at the first call of *any slight irritation.*

As an *exciting* cause of skin diseases in those *predisposed* to them Cow-pox, is *inferior* to other eruptive fevers such as Small-pox, Measles, Scarlatina and Chicken-pox. Sometimes most unmanageable chronic skin diseases follow Small-pox.

It should be borne in mind that certain *hereditary blood diseases* generally produce affections of the skin *for the first time* about the period when Vaccination is usually practised.

Healthy children have been vaccinated from children *known to be diseased in various ways* without the former being in any way affected. M.M. Guersant and Blanche assert that M. Taupin vaccinated a large number of young people at the Children's Hospital in Paris with vaccine lymph taken from subjects affected with Itch, Scarlatina, Measles, Chicken-pox, Small-pox, Rickets, Scrofula, Consumtion, and various skin diseases, &c., without communicating to the patient any of these affections.

Notwithstanding this evidence, no medical man desirous of avoiding future reproach, would vaccinate from children affected with any constitutional or skin disease.

Cow-pox and Small-pox may co-exist. But the contagious matter of each is confined to the vesicle wherein it is developed.

In the following case *a Small-pox pustule* was developed *in the centre of a vaccine vesicle.* Though in such close

contact, each pock contained only its own specific contagion. " A child who had been exposed to the infection of
Small-pox was vaccinated. Both diseases advanced. A
lancet charged with lymph from the vaccine vesicle produced Cow-pox. Another lancet charged with matter from
a Small-pox pustule formed within the vaccine vesicle communicated Small-pox." (*Gregory*.)

M. Bousquet states that Professor Leroux has seen a
vaccine pock implanted *in the centre of a Small-pox
pock*. " He separately inoculated the two viruses ; Vaccination produced Cow-pox with all its advantages, and
Variolation* produced Small-pox with all its dangers."

It may be argued from this, that the ill-defined causes of
constitutional disorders *may also be kept separate* from the
vaccine lymph, and may thus *escape transmission*. It cannot be denied that Cow-pox, like any of the disorders of infancy, may, in *rare* instances, endanger life, or, by being the
exciting cause of the local development of constitutional
disorders, may leave permanent impairment of health, especially in the form of skin and other scrofulous affections.
But these unwelcome results are *as nothing* in the scale
against the immense evils prevented by Vaccination.

The foregoing conclusions are supported by the testi-
mony of medical men possessing large experience of the results of Vaccination.

Sir W. Jenner, Physician in ordinary to Her Majesty, and,
for many years, Physician to the Hospital for Sick Children,
Great Ormond-street, and to University College Hospital—

---

* *i. e.* inoculation of Small-pox.

is of opinion that in no case has he reason to believe, or even to suspect, that any constitutional taint has been conveyed from one person to another by Vaccination.

Mr Paget of St. Bartholomew's Hospital, referring to the causes which develop skin diseases in children observes :— "Now Vaccination may do, though it very rarely does, what these several accidents may do, namely, by disturbing for a time the general health, it may give opportunity for the external manifestation and complete evolution of some constitutional affection, which, but for it, might have remained rather longer latent. This is the worst thing that can with any show of reason be charged against Vaccination ; even this can seldom be charged with truth."

"Scrofula and Rickets cannot be transmitted by Vaccination."—(*Vogel.*)

" The hypothesis that Scrofula was transferred by the Vaccination, from one child to the other, is false. Sometimes children become scrofulous after Vaccination, although the lymph has been taken from the arm of a perfectly healthy child ; and sometimes children remain perfectly healthy after being vaccinated with lymph from a decidedly scrofulous child."—(*Neimeyer.*)

"There is, indeed, no evidence whatever to show that the lymph derived from a typical vaccine eruption, in an apparently healthy child, can possibly be the means of transmitting any constitutional disease."—(*Meigs and Pepper.*)

Mr Marson (who has performed 60,000 Vaccinations) says :—"I have never seen other diseases communicated with the vaccine disease, nor do I believe in the popular reports that they are so communicated."

III.—THE REDUCTION OF SMALL-POX COUNTER-BALANCED BY THE SUBSTITUTION OF OTHER DISEASES.

It is believed by some that humanity always pays the debt of disease and death according to an inevitable law, by which the aggregate amount of them is regulated in proportion to the population. A reduction of the prevalence and death-rate of *one disease*, or *class of diseases*, may not diminish *the sum of sickness and mortality*, because it may then be maintained by an increase of other diseases. It is asserted that Small-pox controlled by Vaccination has been supplanted by :—

　　　　(1) Scrofula.
　　　　(2) Fevers, (especially Typhoid).
　　　　(3) Diphtheria.
　　　　(4) Diseases of Childhood.

1. *Scrofula.*—This constitutional disorder has more of a *fatal* tendency than other chronic diseases, and the mortality of it has undergone remarkable *diminution* since Vaccination has been extensively practised.

2. *Fevers.*—Drs. Farr and Greenhow have proved a great *reduction* in the mortality from fevers since Vaccination was introduced. *Typhoid* Fever is said to be not only more prevalent now than it was prior to Vaccination, but *to be the contagion of Small-pox* developed in another form. If the latter opinion were true, those who had passed through Typhoid would not take Small-

pox—a supposition wholly opposed to experience ; as, according to the following observations (recorded by Dr. Paget, of Cambridge), Typhoid Fever may *remove* the inaptitude for Vaccination left by previous Vaccination, or by Small-pox, it may likewise *favour* rather than *oppose* attacks of this disease. At Swavesey, a populous village in Cambridge, Typhoid Fever was very prevalent and severe in the year 1850. In 1865, on the occurrence of a few cases of Small-pox, the inhabitants, in alarm, young and old alike, sought for Vaccination. Mr. Daniell, the resident surgeon, noticed the remarkable fact, *that the cases of successful Vaccination, in those who had been already vaccinated, or had had Small-pox, were chiefly or almost wholly, among persons who had had Typhoid Fever in* 1850. One was a woman aged 60, whose face was pitted with the Small-pox of twenty years previous. The Vaccination with her proceeded quite normally. She had had Typhoid Fever severely in 1850. Inasmuch as Typhoid Fever may remove the protection afforded by Vaccination, those recently re-covered from it should be re-vaccinated

Epidemics of Typhoid were prevalent long before Vaccination was extensively practised.—(*Stoll, Pinel, Prost*).

3. *Diphtheria.*—It is asserted that this disease was unknown until after Vaccination was introduced. It was described by authors of remote antiquity :—the name is modern,—the disease is ancient. Iretæus called it the Syrian and Egyptian disease, because it was very com-

mon in Syria and Egypt.   In the sixteenth century fearful epidemics of it devastated Spain and Italy, and 100 years ago it was very prevalent in France, Sweden, Germany, and America.   In the year 1855 this disease was for the first time distinguished by the name " Diphtheria" in the Registrar-General's reports.   Since that year, it is believed to have produced a higher mortality than previously;   an impression which may be thus accounted for :—

(1.) Increased knowledge enabling medical men to discriminate between it and allied diseases, such as Croup.

(2.) The greater prevalence being only a rising epidemic wave, to be succeeded by a corresponding fall : similar to the waves of increase and decrease, which have hitherto characterized all infectious diseases.

(3.) A growing population—in part saved from Small-pox by Vaccination—furnishing abundant material for the spread of the disease.

4. *Diseases of Childhood.*—Dr. Farr, in the report of the Registrar-General, 1869, asserts that since the year 1853, the mortality of children has not declined in a degree corresponding with the diminution of Small-pox; other diseases having so prevailed as to reduce the Small-pox gain.   Children *saved from death by Small-pox* may be seized and carried off by other disorders, such as Measles, Scarlatina, Hooping-cough, &c.; for the germs of infectious diseases exist everywhere—in the air we breathe, in the food we eat, and in the water we drink— living germs, ready to reproduce their like on fitting

soil,—to pasture on the bodies of those who supply the material for their development. " Thus in a garden where the flowers are neglected to keep off thistledown, merely leaves the ground open to the world of surrounding weeds."—(*Farr.*)

Inasmuch as the diseases which may flourish among children preserved from Small-pox are *far less fatal*, and *much more under control by ordinary sanitary precautions* than this malignant disease, the mortality they produce does not, by any means, counterbalance the Small-pox gain. We should, therefore, afford protection by Vaccination against one of the most deadly of diseases—Small-pox,—and *at the same time* carry on the work of suppression of other infectious diseases, by wielding the most approved sanitary measures against them *all*. In this way the mortality of our child population will be effectually diminished.

The following question was submitted by the medical officer of the Privy Council to 542 medical men : — " Have you any reason to believe, or to suspect, that vaccinated persons in being rendered less susceptible of Small-pox, become more susceptible of any other infective disease, or of phthisis ; or that their health is in any other way disadvantageously affected ? " Without exception a reply in the negative was returned.

A comparison of the death-rate from all causes *before*, with that *after* the introduction of Vaccination reveals a great improvement of the public health. The supposed substitution of other deaths for those of Small-pox is thus disproved.

In London,   DEATH RATE.

  Middle of last century, 1 in 28 of the population.

  ,,   present century, 1 in 40   ,,

In Sweden,

  from 1750 to 1775, 1 in 35 of the population.

  ,, 1841 to 1850, 1 in 49   ,,   ,,

In London, the death-rate *(excluding Small-pox)* at the middle of last century, was *one-fourth greater* than that *(including Small-pox)* at the middle of this century. "In the first half of the 18th century, the proportion of deaths to births in London, was as 3 to 2, but since 1800, the number of deaths is less than that of births, as 12 to 15."—*(Brigham.)* The statistics of other countries also indicate a great reduction of mortality since the discovery of Vaccination.

The gain pertains *to all periods of life*, and in particular to the years between 20 and 40—a period said to be most fruitful of death in the vaccinated, from those causes supposed to have supplanted Small-pox. "The mortality of early life, and at all ages short of old age, has steadily diminished, and the number of persons who attain a good old age has, as regularly, increased." —*(Seaton.)* Scientific men, and actuaries of assurance offices, are of opinion that the value of life has much increased since the last century, and they believe it is still increasing. This desirable result is due to the application of those sanitary measures shown by experience to be capable of preventing diseases, or of arresting their progress. It cannot be attributed solely to the practice of Vaccination, which is only a specific against Small-pox, and diseases resulting from it. Ordinary sanitary precautions may limit the spread and mortality of infectious disorders, possessing *less* malignity than Small-pox, but, *unaided by efficient Vaccination* they are almost powerless to control this disease. It has, during a period of 70 years, saved, in this country alone, about 5½ millions of lives,* and *no substitute for it being known,* the fearful consequences of its abolition —judging from past experience—can only be imagined ; but they may well deter all but the most rash and ignorant from entertaining such a hazardous experiment. The *most preventable* would then become the *least preventable* of diseases.

IV.—THE PRESUMED INFERIORITY OF THE ORDINARY MODE OF VACCINATION

FROM ARM TO ARM COMPARED WITH VACCINATION FROM THE COW.

It is asserted that Vaccination from the cow is preferable, because:—

1. It is more efficacious than from arm to arm.

2. The possibility of communicating diseases by Vaccination is obviated.

There is some evidence to show that vaccine lymph

---

* "The beneficial influence of Dr. Jenner's immortal discovery saves from death from Small-pox, in our present population in Great Britain, probably about 80,000 lives yearly."—(*Sir J. Simpson.*)

transmitted through many generations* from arm to arm has lost in a slight degree its specific protecting influence. Hence, it is suggested we should revert to the Cow, and substitute that method of Vaccination for the one now in use. To do this, is, however, almost impracticable, because :—

1. It is very difficult to obtain successful Vaccination *direct* from the Cow. The operation has sometimes to be repeated very often before it is successful. When Small-pox is epidemic a most dangerous delay may thus arise,—especially when the Jennerian, or arm-to-arm mode of Vaccination has been discarded. This was the case in France when the recent epidemic broke out. The population was unprepared for the visitation. In Paris systematic Vaccination from arm-to-arm had been to a large extent abandoned for Vaccination from the heifer, which was represented as sufficient for any emergency. When Small-pox began to spread with energy and rapidity, a 'Vaccination panic' arose; ordinary vaccine lymph was no longer obtainable; and the vexatious delay, occasioned by repeated failures of Vaccination from the heifer, permitted the epidemic to advance with unabated fury. The boasted substitute, *even in the hands of its very champions*, failed. "Vaccination after Vaccination has been performed without any effect under circumstances in which human lymph if it could have been obtained would have been certain to succeed. The failures of M.M. Lanoix and of Constantine Paul were 12

---

* This is used in the Medical sense.

out of 13 Vaccinations. Re-vaccinations of the French Soldiers with lymph from the heifer were successful in 16 per cent only as compared with 60 per cent of those with human lymph in the Prussian army."—(*Paris correspondent of Medical Times and Gazette.*

2. The great difficulty of *preserving* Vaccine lymph taken from the cow would necessitate the maintenance of a cumbrous and expensive machinery:—for a newly-vaccinated heifer would have to be provided every week in each district.

3. The possibility of conveying the fatal diseases— Glanders and Farcey—from the heifer to man has been proved.

4. Vaccination from the cow is apt to set up great irritation of the vaccinated part, and much fever : life has thus been endangered.

Vaccination from arm-to-arm possesses the following advantages.

1. It is performed without difficulty and danger.

2. Human lymph may be preserved for months or even years. It may be sent to all parts of the world without impairment of its energy.

The contagion of Small-pox can be so altered by the system of the cow as to be transformed into that of Cow-pox. In like manner vaccine lymph from the cow, introduced into the human system, may be *modified* by the transmission, and *in consequence may be more easily propagated*. This is the chief merit of Jenner's discovery. A common impression prevailed from time immemorial that those who took Cow-pox *from the cow* were preserved from Small-pox; Jenner went further than this: he not only successfully inoculated Cow-pox into the human subject, and thus—proving the correctness of the popular notion—afforded protection from Small-pox, but he transmitted the disease thus established through *a succession of persons*, and it then became so modified—humanized—that the contagion of it—the lymph—could not only be *easily* implanted with success, but could be *preserved* for future use. To abandon arm-to-arm Vaccination for Vaccination from the cow would be to revert to the popular notion respecting Cow-pox which prevailed before the time of Jenner, and to discard the advance made by this acute observer in the immortal discovery by which he *utilized* Cow-pox for the good of mankind.

3. With ordinary care the risk of conveying diseases is so small, that it cannot be compared with the advantages of this mode of Vaccination.

4. It sets up less local and general irritation than Vaccination from the heifer; hence, it is less apt to excite the local development of constitutional disorders existing in the vaccinated.

The only objection which may be urged with truth against the Jennerian mode of Vaccination is the slight impairment of the specific energy of the lymph. It may, however, be restored :—

1. By occasionally, or at stated intervals, reverting to the cow.

2.—By always taking lymph of the *best* quality, and propagating it through the *most healthy* subjects. This process of 'artificial selection' may favour the development of the peculiar properties of the lymph in a manner similar to that adopted by horticulturists when they obtain the best varieties of plants, by always sowing chosen seed in chosen soil.

This position is supported by the following observations :—

Lymph taken from children in unsound or weak health becomes very feeble, especially in the third generation (*Truchetet*) ; conversely, it may be anticipated, that when passed through a succession of very healthy children, it may become stronger. Professor Trousseau showed by observations made in the Hôtel Dieu that vaccine lymph may be *regenerated* by selecting the best specimens and transmitting them through the most healthy subjects. " We vaccinated a healthy child ; we took matter on the fourth or fifth day from this child, and transmitted it to other children in the best possible state of health. After a certain number of generations, the lymph appeared to us to have become more energetic, to manifest its effects more quickly, and to take a longer time to complete its evolution, * than the lymph with which we commenced the series of Vaccinations. Not wishing to put too much reliance on our impressions, a child was sent to the *Mairie* of the eleventh *Arondisement* to be vaccinated. On the eighth day, lymph

* Indicating increased strength of the lymph.

was taken from this child, and with it the left arm of a healthy child was vaccinated, while, at the same time, the right arm was vaccinated with lymph taken from a subject in our wards. Several other children were vaccinated in the same manner, and our impression was that our 'regenerated lymph' was more energetic than the lymph used in the town."—*(Chinique Medical.)*

Two practial lessons are taught by these facts :—

1.   For supplying lymph, children in vigorous health should be selected, because there will be less suspicion of the communication of diseases, and the lymph will be more energetic. and afford better protection, than when taken from less healthy subjects.

2.   To enable the vaccinator to use on all occasions good active lymph, parents of healthy children should regard it a *duty* to permit him to take a proper supply. It is much to be regretted they not unfrequently refuse this,—forgetting how they thus impede efficient Vaccination, and may be compel the vaccinator to procure lymph from less healthy subjects.

Injurious effects do not, as a rule, arise from the removal of lymph.

CONCLUSIONS.

1. Vaccination greatly diminishes the probabilities of an attack of Small-pox, and, when properly performed, is an almost absolute security against death from this disease.

2. Vaccination has greatly diminished the frequency and fatality of epidemics of Small-pox.

3. The protecting power of Vaccination against Small-pox is *not absolute*. The properly vaccinated occasionally catch this disease: but their liability diminishes in proportion to the efficiency of previous Vaccination, and is almost *nil* after re-vaccination.

4. When Small-pox seizes the UNVACCINATED, it does so severely, and the average mortality is from 35 to 40 per cent.; those who recover are greatly disfigured; sometimes sight and hearing are lost, or seriously impaired; and occasionally the health is permanently damaged. When it affects the VACCINATED, as a rule the attack is mild, and the mortality from $\frac{1}{2}$ to 8 per cent.: according to the efficiency of Vaccination; disfigurement is the exception; loss or impairment of sight or hearing exceedingly rare; and permanent injury to health very uncommon.

5. Re-vaccination at the age of puberty is *as necessary*, and should therefore be performed *as systematically* as primary Vaccination.

6. There is no evidence to prove that, as a rule, Vaccination affects the health more injuriously than do the ordinary infectious disorders of childhood.

7. The remarkable reduction of the mortality from Small-pox, resulting from the benign influence of Vaccination, is not counterbalanced by increased death-rate of other diseases.

8. The ordinary (or Jennerian) mode of Vaccination from arm to arm *is preferable* to Vaccination from the cow.

9. Vaccination is a *national* blessing. The wealth of a nation is its people. It is estimated that in this country more than 80,000 lives are annually preserved by Vaccination. Malignant Small-pox, by bereaving wives and children, and by inflicting the distressing calamity of blindness* (thus transforming valuable lives into useless ones), increases the unproductive class—mendicants and paupers—supported by those who are the life and energy of society. In this way it diverts to unprofitable ends, resources which should be applied to the attainment of social advantages and the prosperity of the nation. Inasmuch as experience proves Vaccination to be a harmless and reliable shield against the *national* calamity of uncontrolled Small-pox, it is the duty of the legislature

---

* It is estimated that before Vaccination was practised *two thirds* of he blind of this country owed their terrible calamity to Small-pox.

to enforce its application irrespective of the opposition of those who are either uninformed, or who refuse to be instructed by facts.

10.   Vaccination is a *personal* blessing.   It prevents much misery and deformity ; it increases the security and the average duration of life.

11.   Refusal to undergo Vaccination involves great responsibility.   Small-pox usually selects the non-vacci-nated as its first victims ; safety being only secured by absence of the contagion,—their lives, however valuable, are exposed to imminent danger—especially when the disease is epidemic.   When non-vaccinated children are seized and carried off by it, parents or guardians are culpable.   To forego Vaccination is not a matter of mere *individual* responsibility ; the lives of others—even those of the vaccinated—are imperilled thereby.   The non-vaccinated are dangerous to society, because they encourage the spread of malignant Small-pox, and they, suffering from the worst form of the disease, generate a most deadly contagion.

12.   Opposition to Vaccination is pernicious, because it encourages a return of a deadly evil from the thraldom of which the civilized world has, in a great measure, been relieved ; and it is apt to engender doubt when, according to indisputable evidence, there should be the strongest faith and confidence concerning the benefits conferred on humanity, by one of the greatest discoveries of medical science.

Vaccination is proved by the most positive evidence to be a great and singular blessing, in shielding us from the fatal assaults of a most loathsome and terrible disease. Surely this unique act of mercy in the Creator should inspire us with feelings of gratitude and thankfulness.

ADDENDUM.

SMALL-POX HOSPITAL, HAMPSTEAD.

Admissions :—(to Feb. 4th, 1871) 582.

Vaccinated :—423.   Deaths, 29, or 7 per cent.

Non Vaccinated :—159.   Deaths, 68, or 43 per cent.

Average duration of attacks.

Vaccinated : 23 days.

Non-vaccinated : 34 days.

Dr. Greave, the Medical Officer, finds, according to the statistics relating to the present epidemic, the number of the *unvaccinated* patients up to the age of 10 years greatly preponderates over the *vaccinated* of corrèsponding ages. Beyond that period of life, it diminishes, until at the age of 40 years, only 4 *unvaccinated* persons are admitted.

REDCAR :

G. F. BATES, PRINTER.